The Martians Have Landed

SCHOLASTIC INC.

New York Toronto London Auckland Sydney
Mexico City New Delhi Hong Kong Buenos Aires

Written by
Gerry Bailey

No part of this work may be reproduced in whole or in part, or stored in a retrieval system, or transmitted in any form or by any means, electronic, mechanical, photocopying, recording, or otherwise, without the written permission of the publisher. For information regarding permission, write to Scholastic Inc., Attention: Permissions Department, 555 Broadway, New York, NY 10012.

ISBN   0-439-37027-2

Produced by Scholastic Inc. in 2001 under license from Just Licensing Ltd. © 2000 Just Entertainment Ltd/Mike Young Productions Inc/Digital Content Development Corporation Ltd.

Published by Scholastic Inc. SCHOLASTIC and associated logos are trademarks and/or registered trademarks of Scholastic Inc.

12 11 10 9 8 7 6 5 4 3 2   1 2 3 4 5 6/0

Printed in the U.S.A.
First Scholastic printing, December 2001

It is the year 2053. Kids are eating burgers, Moms and Dads are at work — or doing whatever it is that Moms and Dads do — and everything is fine in the solar system. But it isn't! Far out in space, drifting among the asteroids, are the lethal battle cruisers of the deadly Martian Emperor, Bog.

Many years ago, Mars was made uninhabitable as a result of an incident the Martians simply refer to as "Oops." They need a new home, and the emperor has his eye on Earth.

Nothing is going to stand in his way. Emperor Bog plans to invade Earth using his Martian troops — but first he decides to send a small advance force to soften up the enemy! But who is going to go? A competition is organized to choose the Martians who will receive this rare and dangerous honor.

Aboard the emperor's battle cruiser, the *Bogstar*, preparations for the competition begin. . . .

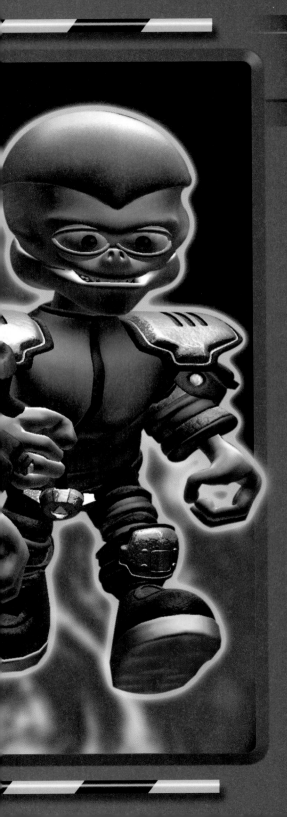

Three of the Martians are determined to be selected. They are already studying the planet that their emperor is desperate to conquer. They have even given themselves Earth-type names based on music they've heard coming from the blue planet.

"Wow," said Trooper Do-Wah-Diddy, "Earth is just about the coolest place in the universe. All that music, food, and TV. . . ."

"Yeah, yeah," said Commander B.Bop-A-Luna, "we all love the place, but it won't be Earth anymore once Emperor Bog gets through with it."

"Then there's only one thing to do," said Tech Commando 2-T-Fru-T. "And that is to use dubious tactics in the competition."

"You mean cheat?" said B.Bop.

"Sure do, babe!" said 2-T. "I'm sure Bog won't notice a little reality-bending. . . ."

7

Emperor Bog was impatient. The competition was over, and he had found his three finest Martian troopers. Only, they didn't exactly look the part, especially the one called Do-Wah.

"How in my name did these three win?" said Emperor Bog to Dr. Damage, his science officer and all-around henchman.

"I'm completely in the dark," said Damage.

Bog addressed the three troopers: "I want this job done quickly and efficiently. The penalty for failure is death. The penalty for near failure is death. The penalty for taking too long is death. The penalty for — "

"Very good my liege," broke in Damage. "But the troops must depart and I must prepare my lab for Earthling experiments. I can hardly wait!"

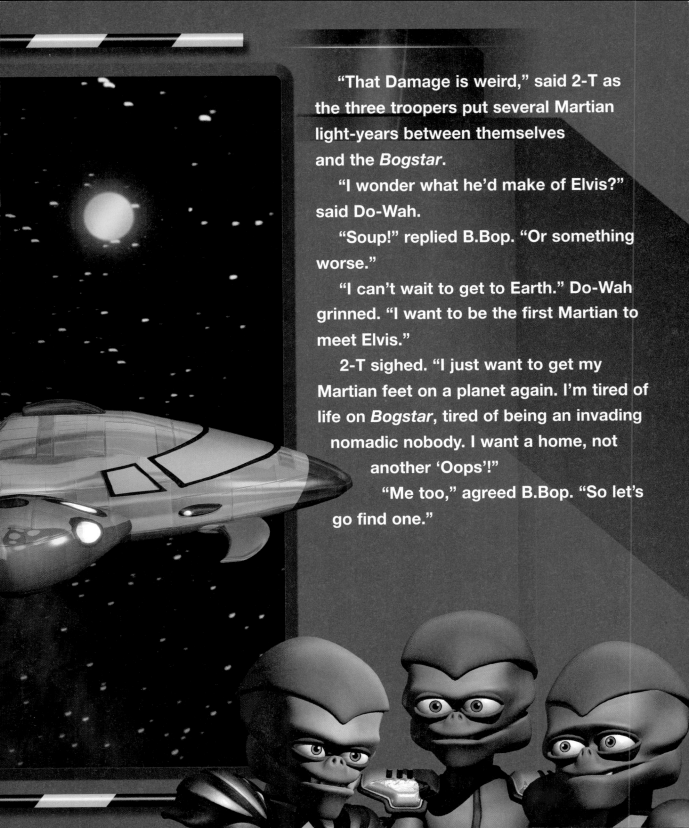

"That Damage is weird," said 2-T as the three troopers put several Martian light-years between themselves and the *Bogstar*.

"I wonder what he'd make of Elvis?" said Do-Wah.

"Soup!" replied B.Bop. "Or something worse."

"I can't wait to get to Earth." Do-Wah grinned. "I want to be the first Martian to meet Elvis."

2-T sighed. "I just want to get my Martian feet on a planet again. I'm tired of life on *Bogstar*, tired of being an invading nomadic nobody. I want a home, not another 'Oops'!"

"Me too," agreed B.Bop. "So let's go find one."

Meanwhile on Earth, in an unused missile silo somewhere in the Mojave Desert, vigilant eyes scanned the heavens, watching for signs of alien movement. The eyes belonged to Stoat Muldoon: Alien Hunter. In his role as chief investigative agent for paranormal events, Stoat Muldoon zeroed in on an unknown spacecraft heading for Earth.

"This is it," he muttered. "Alien scum, you've met your match. Prepare to face Stoat Muldoon. What the. . . snow in the Mojave Desert! That hasn't happened since the Eccles Incident in 2043! Brrrr. . . I still have frostbite on my pinkie!"

In fact, there was no snow. Fixed to the top of Muldoon's base was a huge satellite dish. While it worked well for tracking space stuff, three kids found it much more useful as a takeoff point for their hoverboard stunts.

Mike, Angela, and Cedric often came here to test their skills, but so far they hadn't noticed the presence of the mighty alien hunter. That was about to change.

"Hey Ange, get a load of this — a 540 wingswagger!" yelled Mike as he took off from the dish and performed the stunt perfectly. Angela launched herself into the air and copied Mike's stunt.

"Too cool!" said Cedric.

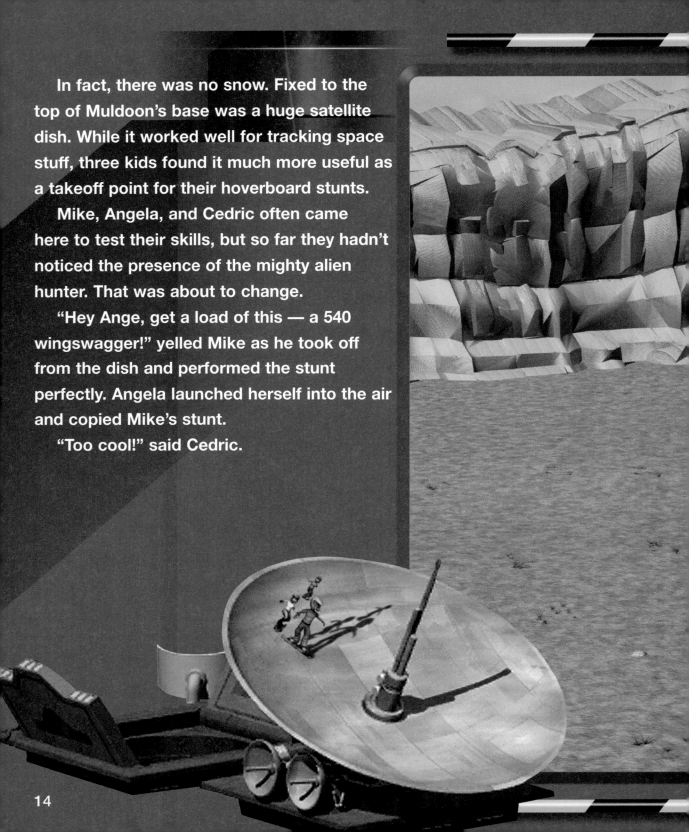

Muldoon's screen was scattered with static and the picture was beginning to break up.

"Wait! That's not snow. Someone is messing with my digitals."

He rushed out of the silo and looked around until his eyes rested on the satellite dish. The cause of the interference was right in front of him — not aliens, but kids.

"Youngsters playing on the dish. They have no idea that Earth is being invaded! Get off, children!" yelled Muldoon.

Angela turned as she heard a voice she recognized. "It's that weirdo alien hunter from TV and the Internet!" she yelled. "Let's get out of here!"

Muldoon jumped in his hovervan and chased after the kids. Rounding them up wasn't an easy job, however.

"Children! Stop! We're facing an invasion from possible hostile aliens. It's not safe out here!"

He was about to close in when a flash of light and a rush of energy stopped him cold. His MATD (Multipurpose Alien Tracking Device) sounded a loud alarm.

Muldoon swung the hovervan around. "I've hit pay dirt! Those kids will have to wait!" With that, Muldoon prepared his tractor beam to use on the new arrivals. . . .

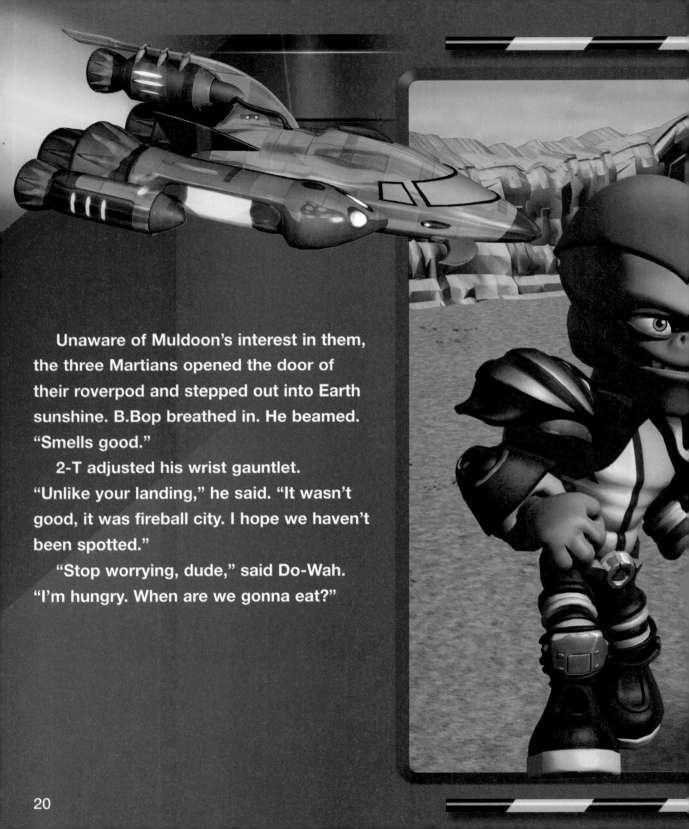

Unaware of Muldoon's interest in them, the three Martians opened the door of their roverpod and stepped out into Earth sunshine. B.Bop breathed in. He beamed. "Smells good."

2-T adjusted his wrist gauntlet. "Unlike your landing," he said. "It wasn't good, it was fireball city. I hope we haven't been spotted."

"Stop worrying, dude," said Do-Wah. "I'm hungry. When are we gonna eat?"

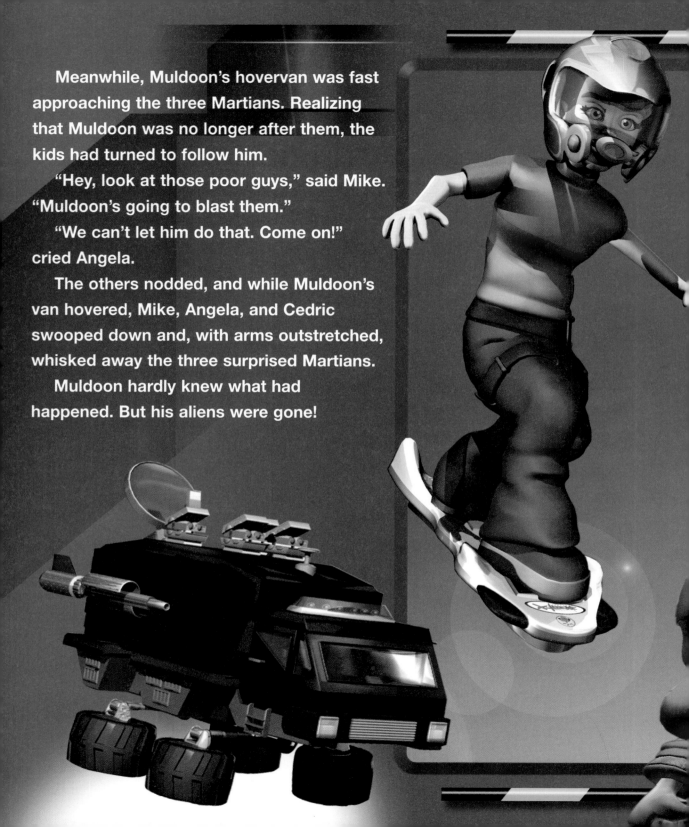

Meanwhile, Muldoon's hovervan was fast approaching the three Martians. Realizing that Muldoon was no longer after them, the kids had turned to follow him.

"Hey, look at those poor guys," said Mike. "Muldoon's going to blast them."

"We can't let him do that. Come on!" cried Angela.

The others nodded, and while Muldoon's van hovered, Mike, Angela, and Cedric swooped down and, with arms outstretched, whisked away the three surprised Martians.

Muldoon hardly knew what had happened. But his aliens were gone!

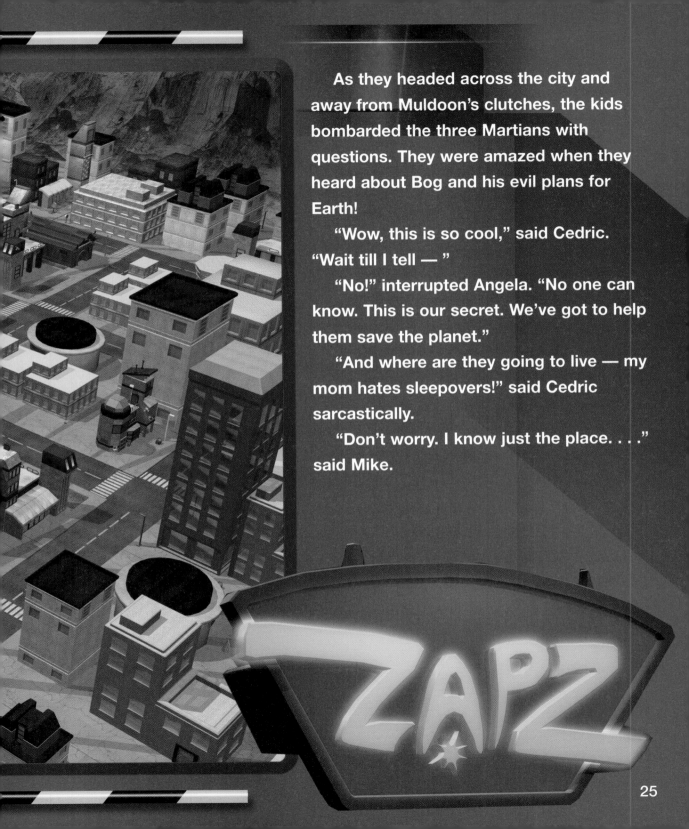

As they headed across the city and away from Muldoon's clutches, the kids bombarded the three Martians with questions. They were amazed when they heard about Bog and his evil plans for Earth!

"Wow, this is so cool," said Cedric. "Wait till I tell — "

"No!" interrupted Angela. "No one can know. This is our secret. We've got to help them save the planet."

"And where are they going to live — my mom hates sleepovers!" said Cedric sarcastically.

"Don't worry. I know just the place. . . ." said Mike.

"Here it is!" cried Mike as the three hoverboards banked across an old area of the city.

"Looks good to me Mikey, but what is it?" asked B.Bop.

"It's an old arcade," said Angela. "It was closed down around 2001. It's full of old games that don't work anymore."

"No problem, babe," said 2-T. "They'll work when I've finished with them."

Once inside, the Martians made themselves at home. Mike watched and grinned. "Wow, are they ugly," he whispered to Angela.

"Butt-ugly," she giggled.

2-T looked over the games and began to get his own tech area together. Quickly, he got to work on something he'd been developing back on the *Bogstar*. "This canine-looking electronic object is Dog." He grinned. "He will be our scout and protector. . . ."

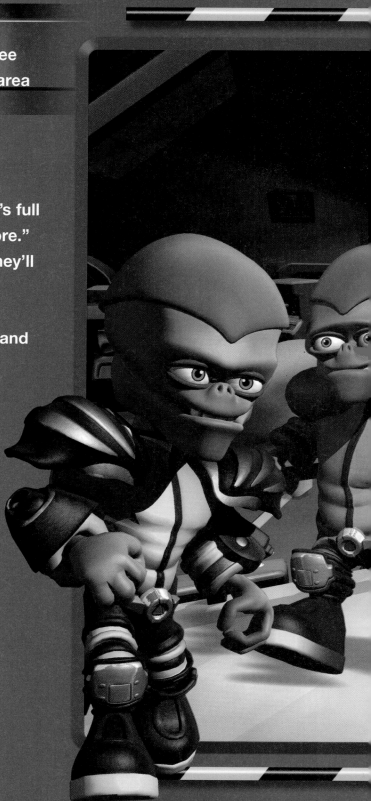

Suddenly Cedric had a thought. He looked at the Martians and asked, "And just how are three little guys like you going to stop an emperor, or even a Stoat Muldoon, come to that?"

Angela started to speak, but 2-T broke in. "No problem, babe. We've been working on something Bog knows nothing about."

"And he must *never* know," said B.Bop. "Just watch this."

The three Martians chanted, "B! K! M!" Then they shouted, "LET'S GET UGLY!"

And to the kids' delight they showed just how awesome they really could be.

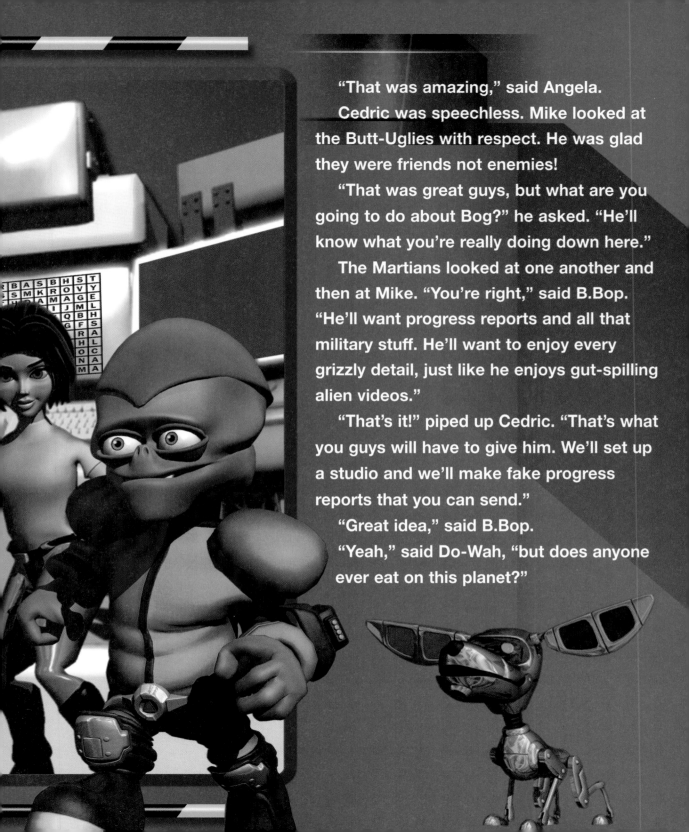

"That was amazing," said Angela.

Cedric was speechless. Mike looked at the Butt-Uglies with respect. He was glad they were friends not enemies!

"That was great guys, but what are you going to do about Bog?" he asked. "He'll know what you're really doing down here."

The Martians looked at one another and then at Mike. "You're right," said B.Bop. "He'll want progress reports and all that military stuff. He'll want to enjoy every grizzly detail, just like he enjoys gut-spilling alien videos."

"That's it!" piped up Cedric. "That's what you guys will have to give him. We'll set up a studio and we'll make fake progress reports that you can send."

"Great idea," said B.Bop.

"Yeah," said Do-Wah, "but does anyone ever eat on this planet?"

LET'S GET UGLY!